Overcoming Narcissistic Relationships as an Empath

Breaking Karmic Cycles of Empaths & Narcissists

Jade Asikiwe

© 2020

COPYRIGHT

Overcoming Narcissistic Relationships as an Empath

By Jade Asikiwe

TABLE OF CONTENTS

Chapter 1: Empaths & Narcissists

Empaths and narcissists. Two extremely different personalities that some may consider to be opposites. It can be hard to picture an empath and a narcissist in the same relationship, but it happens way often, especially in today's dating culture. As we dive into the true inner workings of these two vastly different types of people, you will see how their personalities are almost tailor-made for each-other... and not usually ideal for the best overall outcome. Let us begin with empaths.

An empath is someone that has a great amount of empathy and emotion. They sense energy in many forms and feel things on a much deeper level. Empaths also have a strong intuition and are sometimes able to sense things before they happen. They are naturally in-tune with nature, and the cosmic forces that give them the ability to have heightened intuition and the ability to read energy in other people.

Empaths are known to be very giving, loving, selfless people, and will, in most cases, put someone else's needs ahead of their own. There are many people who are unaware that they are an empath and they may come off in life as very timid and scared to speak their mind. An empath may seem as if they are afraid to be around people and be confident. They may experience a great deal of energy and mood swings that can be based solely on their environment; they may not understand what is going on within them, but there is possibly much more at play there

Empaths rarely just experience emotion, they truly feel it: more than a mental attribute, some empathic people physically feel the ups and downs of emotional release. Emotion is a very intense occurrence for empaths, and events and situations in life that may be easily digestible to others, may be overwhelming and hurtful to an empath. Empaths are extraordinarily strong, but also very fragile and precious. They feel emotion on a very deep level, so words and actions will have a totally different effect on an empath. Empaths not only feel the emotions of themselves or others, but they empathize with those around them- the root of the word is the same. They feel sorry for the most wretched of souls, and often feel everyone is worthy of love and help. Empaths harbor the ability to put themselves in someone's shoes and truly feel their pain and will try and do all they can to help a person through their struggle. Natural healers. Selflessness is one of the biggest qualities that you can find in an empath.

Narcissists, on the other hand, are completely opposite. I will keep this description brief because we will get into the very detailed definition and explanation of narcissism also known as NPD, Narcissistic Personality Disorder but let's lay out the simple known facts about what we know about narcissists so we can see the contrast between the personality of an empath. Narcissists are the exact opposite of an empath. They are known to be selfish and self-serving, with little to no regard for another person's thoughts and feelings. They have an inflated ego and major sense of self and mastery over confidence.

A narcissist's first thought is not usually about another person or the needs of others- it is usually centered on themselves. An empath is always thinking of other people and feeling the weight of the world on their shoulders. They want to help everyone and save the world.

Empaths feel a very deep and in tune level of emotion so with all the injustices and abuses that happen each day in the world, they must endure it in a much different way. So, you can see the obvious differences within the two personalities that we have here. Let us go into the dating phase and see how a relationship like this begins.

Chapter 2: (Dating a Narcissist: The Viewpoint of an Empath)

You meet this person, maybe by accident, maybe not. This magical person you meet is very calculated, which is why I said, "maybe by accident, or maybe not". This is the romance, the fun, the glitz, the glamour phase. You meet this incredible person and they seem to be literally everything that you ever dreamed of.

The romantic nights out are so well thought out, they seem to truly invest their time, energy, emotions, thoughts, feelings, being into you. They may even be asking a lot of questions that you haven't even really thought about yourself, but it feels so refreshing to talk about the things that you value or have been through, so nice to get things off of our chest that we don't even see the danger of over-sharing, so you keep telling them all of these vulnerable things about yourself. You keep right on talking and confiding in them, sense of security comforted. During this time, you are bombarded with gifts, and an almost overwhelming amount of attention and affection. This is all part of the "luring-in" process, or what can be known as "love bombing".

There is a certain alluring mystery that a defined narcissist has. The reason a can become so captivated by a narcissist during this time is believed to be a combination of several things: a big ego, lots of charm, and a massive amount of confidence. This charming, charismatic and mysterious behavior may be something some people find intriguing, bold, and exciting. They love a narcissist's confidence and ability to be bold.

You are being wined and dined. Given special attention and the word "love" is somehow used incredibly early in the relationship. It may seem as if everything was bland, lifeless and colorless before you met this person, and every person was the same to you; suddenly, you are happier than you have ever been. There may be small things that you are overlooking because you are so "in love", but those "small things" are categorized as red flags. They appear in every relationship, both platonic and romantic; but just like in many other relationships from work, friends, love, and family, red flags often go excused or unaddressed because of how new a situation is, or who that person may be in your life, or- let's be honest- you enjoy the love and attention so much, that you just let it go. However, red flags are signing that we should pay attention to as closely as possible. The sooner, the better.

The red flags can be anything. They are not usually obvious, because if they were, most people would get out well before things take a turn for the worst... but that is not how it often goes. While everything is seeming sweet, there are little things that arise that cross your mind and make you think twice, or maybe you want to say something, but you do not. At this point, their seduction is so strong that you are willing to overlook almost anything. Almost.

Empaths are good at reading energy, as we discussed, but the charms and magic that the narcissist is displaying can really cloud judgement. For instance, it may start with things such as fast marriage proposals, erratic decisions, even as far as the narcissists saying things like they've actually been "watching" you or saying they've had their eye on you for a long time… but that sentence doesn't really register for most victims like it should. Remember, in the very beginning, I said the person is very calculated, and you meet them by accident- or maybe not? That is a huge red flag! You should make a mental note to sound the alarm if that sentence is spoken. Many narcissists study and prey upon their target before they make a move. So, for you, it may have been the first-time meeting or seeing them, but it surely was not their first time seeing you.

Now, since it's still new and flirty; since it seems to be romantic that someone has been eyeing you, while all the while you never knew who they even were; that is actually something to be a tad weary about. An empath may pick up on that, but it still may not sink in until later down the line that it was something, they should have paid attention to. There are other signs or red flags, but still nothing too shocking to walk away from, right? It may even be a slight temper that they have but they hurry up and mask it with an excuse or laugh it off and say it was nothing when actually it's a quick temper that if given the environment would show its true self. But they are not at that stage yet. Of letting you know who they truly are. So, they contain that part...for now.

Depending on who the person is and their personality, other red flags to look for while in the honeymoon, blissful stage, is the slow-and-steady integration of preferences and demands from the narcissists. It may not be anything too big of an issue at first but it may start with how you wear your hair, to what you wear, to what their plans are for the relationship and you'll start seeing how your opinion isn't often asked for by the narcissists in the topic. But again, empaths love to make people happy, and really do not want to cause problems so they may agree to this without giving it real thought.

Big red flags are when your employment / dreams are completely altered or put down by the person you love. Narcissists like to be in control so after time of dating, you may be approached with the idea of quitting your job or just moving a major distance with them and they will be completely oblivious to how much you've given to your career or your passion and they just want you to "let them take care of you." Sound familiar?

Usually when you are seeing someone, you bring them around the family. Let them meet your mom, dad, brothers, sisters, etc. No matter how smooth someone is, there is usually one person out the bunch that spots a red flag from a mile away. Our mothers are exceptionally good at that; sometimes it is family events that you see something, hear something, learn something that you may not have previously known about your new romantic partner. These times can provide a certain amount of clarity and insight because sometimes under pressure of being in front of someone's family, you can see them in a different light.

Again, keep an eye on the friends and family of the narcissist. These people are usually very fond of the narcissist and enable their behavior. You will notice that the narcissist is vastly different from everyone in the family and that they usually carry some sort of attitude of arrogance and authority. The family of a dangerous narcissist is something to be very wary of because they are a part of the abuse that you may experience as well. I call this third-party abuse", which we will discuss in just a little bit.

When narcissists are around a group of people, they tend to need to shine and be the smartest in the room. An empath however may feel the energy in a room and will react based off that. Narcs also may act totally different around your family and other people then they do around you.

Now, of course, everyone in some way or another does that. We act a certain way in public, to protect our projected image, and we become a bit more relaxed around those we can feel personal and vulnerable with… but narcissists take it to a completely different level. They are absurdly genius when it comes to blending in and adapting to their surrounding crowd and can be two completely different people. A monster at home, but practically a Nobel Peace Prize winner, or mother/father of the year in public. When in the dating stage, look out for the Dr. Jekyll and Mr. Hyde pattern of behavior. When they are one way with you and another with other people. Do not brush these actions off as "just stress" or "a one-time thing." That is a major red flag when someone can totally change faces without warning and blame you for it.

For some people, it does not matter how many red flags there are. They are so in-love and infatuated during this stage, that they do not see the possessive, over-confident, selfish shark standing right in front of them. For an empath, who feels everything, they may see every red flag and sense something is off with the energy, but yet, they are still an empath, meaning they deeply care for this individual, so they may be unable to truly see a situation for what it is as it is presented before them. Sooner or later, however, those rose-colored glasses do come off.

Narcissists are controlling and very calculated. They like certainty with near-instant results; they are not fond of chasing you for too long, for it would be risking the chance of "losing you". Eventually, they will pressure you for deep commitment in the relationship, probably sooner than you wanted to. This could mean marriage exceedingly early on, maybe a push for a seriously intimate sexual dynamic. They insist that you should move in with them, things will be easier when you move in, just trust them. They seem to say all the right things and seem to be the person that wants to take care of you, and before you know it, you consider it. A moment of weakness ruins your resolve, and you take the plunge- the moment they were waiting for. You say yes to the ring, you combine households with them, you consent to a deed that makes your stomach churn slightly…. Because they love you. They have told you they would bring the world down for you, and I mean, really, who would not want to hear that? Wouldn't you bring the world down for them, too? Isn't it natural to move on from this stage to the next?

This is the meat-and-potatoes of a narcissistic relationship. Every relationship begins wonderfully, right? When you move in with someone and are around them all day, you are bound to have some complications and some arguments, right? Relationships of all kinds have complications of some kind, be it siblings, friends, parents, and/or romantic relationships. Narcissistic abusive relationships start a tad different than most, however, and are unique in the fact that they may begin like a fairytale, but are very much the opposite of what will happen once the relationship progresses- and it especially affects empaths and emotional beings as a whole in an extreme manner.

The dating phase is important to point out because remember some of the key things that happen when you are dating a narcissist. The red flags, the overconfidence, the fast movement and pressure of the relationship to be more are just some of the things that happen during this time. If you are aware of early signs, you can possibly avoid serious mental trauma and damage.

As we move further in this book, we will see how everything unfolds once we have fallen for the narcissists. We will now move into exactly what the true definition of what a narcissist is, and dive deeper into the mind of someone who thinks and lives in such a calculated manner.

CHAPTER 3: WHAT IS A NARCISSIST?

"Narcissistic Personality Disorder - A disorder in which a person has an inflated sense of self. Narcissistic personality disorder is found more commonly in men. The cause is unknown but likely involves a combination of genetic and environmental factors. Symptoms may include an excessive need for admiration and praise, complete disregard for other people's feeling, lack of empathy, an inability to handle criticism - will claim you are just jealous of them and their life, and a grand sense of entitlement."

Mayo Clinic

Narcissism is not just someone who likes to look at themselves in the mirror and take selfies to post online; it is not someone that just may be tad selfish here and there, but still is loving overall. NPD, or "Narcissist Personality Disorder", is very, very categorized. While new cases only average around 200,000 a year, this can go undiagnosed as it is an invisible disability, meaning that because it isn't an obviously-appearing disorder, it can fly under the radar until the affected person acts in a manner that a doctor can pick up on. NPD affects a great deal of people around the world; it is not something to take lightly, for it causes serious psychological damage to the people around this person if it goes unaddressed.

Several traits of (NPD) - Narcissistic Personality Disorder.

1) Grand sense of entitlement

2) Obsession or Preoccupation with fantasies of unlimited success, power, brilliance, wealth, or beauty

3) A belief that they are God-like and above all other humans

4) Need for excessive admiration

5) Grandiose sense of self-importance

6) Excessive arrogance and haughty attitude

7) Lack of Empathy and emotion or the emotional needs of others.

8) Interpersonally exploitative behavior

9) They think they are just misunderstood

10) They believe they are so special and unique to the point they feel as if they can only be understood by, or should associate with other special high-status people, organizations, and institutions.

11) Envy and jealousy for others or extreme belief that others are jealous of them.

12) Often repeats the same behavior in all relationships but blames the victim.

13) Careless, reckless behavior with no regard to how it affects those around them.

14) Self-absorbed and extreme selfishness

15) Lies

16) Manipulates events, people, and situations to their benefit

Along with the known traits that come with narcissists, it is important to take note that they surround themselves with people that are easily manipulated: those that are gullible, blindly loyal, fans, followers, enablers, and cheerleaders. Their ego is massive, yes- but extremely fragile; One wrong comment could set off an explosive argument. Narcissists do not like anyone around that tries to give them any sort of criticism, when someone tells them how their actions made them feel, and they especially do not like when you remind them of any sort of obligation and or responsibility. They do not think they "have" to do anything.

In Chapter 1, it was mentioned to take notice of the family, friends, and fans that the narcissist has around them. This is important to take note of, because it is not only the narcissist that you will be dealing with, but victims may also experience trauma and mental abuse at the hands of those around and related to the narcissist.

Does any of this sound familiar? Do you perhaps know someone that has these qualities, and/or see them in yourself? Do not be alarmed, it is okay if you do see things that either you or someone you know may need to work on because this book is to help bring those feelings to the surface and help you get through and cope with the effects of narcissism and or narcissistic abuse.

To begin, do not think that because someone may be selfish and a bit overconfident that it immediately deems them a narcissist. That is not true at all; if that were the case, most of the human population would be considered narcissistic. There is a reason that this behavior has an actual name and has been diagnosed as a disorder: narcissists need an extreme- almost unhealthy- amount of praise and propping up. They need to always be right, no matter what and feel nothing when it comes to other people's emotions and tears. There is a certain disconnect when it comes to a narcissist and emotions. A major lack of feeling and empathy.

SOCIOPATHIC TENDENCIES

Another type of person that carries this trait can be known as a sociopath. The definition of a sociopath or Antisocial Personality Disorder is a mental health disorder characterized by a disregard for other people. Those diagnosed with this disorder are said to lie, break laws, act impulsively, and lack regard for their safety or the safety of others. There is a tremendous amount of selfishness involved in this as well. They do not care about the position their decisions put you in and they will say you do not believe in them or trust them if you object and raise your concerns with some of their questionable decisions. That is a manipulation tactic by the way that we will get into shortly.

A narcissist and a sociopath are similar in the way an orange and a clementine are similar: they are the same fruit, but different enough to not be categorized as the same thing. The two often intertwine when referencing manipulation and calculation. There are many well-documented criminals in history diagnosed with these very characteristics. Criminals that have an extreme talent for manipulation and mind games, that have no remorse, or for some reason are unable or simply do not care to see the actual severity of their actions because they in fact do not or absolutely refuse to see it, think they are above the law.

For some, this may sound like a person who just has an inflated sense-of-self while acting recklessly, but the real underlying problems with this behavior are ignored. When you are in a relationship with someone who does not know how to or care to reciprocate half of the things you do for them, it is very one-sided, and difficult to maintain happiness that way. Keep in mind, a narcissist only cares about themselves, so after that sweet phase of dating and putting on the heaven-on-earth façade, their true selves begin to show, and you start to see how selfish and one-sided the relationship really is, so it is important to try and avoid it before any damage is done.

Narcissism is not an adult- only affliction: children and teens/ young adults also are affected by this. You can research stories of parents who have a troubled teen on their hands, and all too often you will read/ hear sentences such as:

"He/She just doesn't care."

"When I cry, my child actually laughs."

"It's as if...my child doesn't have any emotion."

"He/she refuses to take any responsibility."

These are just some of the things that can be commonly heard from spouses, significant others, and parents alike when dealing with someone with narcissistic traits. Thinking back to the definition, narcissism also makes the person feel a huge sense of entitlement, as if the world and everyone in it owes them something. I am not referring to someone that has been through something extremely traumatic and now feels they are perhaps owed for what happened; specifically, this is someone born-and-raised to think with an oh-so-special mindset. Generally, they do not have to work hard or be humble, because they have been coddled and pampered with everything handed to them out of sheer love and admiration for their convenience.

They feel like just because they are who they are, anyone should feel blessed to have them. You are the lucky one, not them. And they love to remind you just how many other people "want your spot"; a smooth manipulating tactic, letting you know that you should always stay on your toes, and treat them perfectly. There is always someone else "begging" to be where you are, as if this person is in just such high-demand- a narcissist in flesh, blood, and phrase. No one is better than them, all humans are beneath them, the world revolves around them, and they rule the Earth.

Though a narcissist may be lacking in emotions and empathy themselves, they certainly know how to play upon these emotions in others. Let us talk mind games, mind control, and manipulation.

MANIPULATION

An often-used tactic by narcissists is mind control and/or mind manipulation. I am not referring to the use of spells or anything like that, just mastery over self. That is what narcissists have in spades. They are very aware of their surroundings, so it makes it easier for them to manipulate when getting to know and learn someone else. That is why they can hide in plain sight and are always watching for the next "target" in their journey through life.

A "Type A" narcissist has the uncanny ability to literally remove things you once held with value and importance and make them either cease to exist or move them to the back burner. Either mental and general thoughts and values you once had, or physical possessions. Somehow everything you have will be given to you by them, and all your things, your home, your car, somehow disappear, and you become completely dependent on them.

Mind games and the art of manipulation have been seen and felt throughout time by the victims of narcissists. The effects of having control over someone are real, and should not be brushed off, nor should anyone ask terrible questions such as, "if it was so bad, why didn't they just leave?" It is not that simple. If no one is threatening your life and or holding you hostage, you should be free to go right? Wrong. So wrong. Mental manipulation, as mentioned above, has been seen throughout time by many men and women who have been through domestic violence and/or mental and narcissistic abuse. Manipulation is a strong way to have someone trauma-bonded to someone else, and that is the goal for the narcissists. It is so that you can be completely dependent on them.

When someone can get in your mind, they could inadvertently control you, your thoughts, and your actions. With that power, they turn your thoughts, values, beliefs, and actions. Manipulation is not usually obvious; it is a covert operation, a hidden attack on your mind, an attempt to sway your thoughts with the goal being to influence the mind in favor of the attacker.

Manipulation is subtle, and whatever the request is from the narcissists may seem as if there is mutual benefit, or the promises they made may have sounded great, but that is all an illusion. They have absolutely no intention of showing genuine love or compassion in a serious relationship, and anything they promised was only out of benefit for them. When under the "spell" or influence of lust and manipulation, your eyes are not fully open. You may be so clouded by the love you have for the narcissist that you fail to see the manipulation, unless you have a trained eye- and sometimes, even that is not always efficient. You are blinded by the charm, the charisma, their promises that you will soon see never actually end up happening. That promise extends the time that you will stay, and not pester them about it, so they just keep right on making promises. There may even be obvious signs that family and/or friends may try to warn you about, but you ignore and make excuses, in fear of losing your perfect bubble. In this dating stage, it is the charm, the animal magnetism, the feeling of being understood that keeps you there. As of this moment, this person can do no wrong in your eyes. But all spells wear off after a while. All things end. Eventually, you will see the charm and technique for what it really is: a lie.

THE LIE

The subtle start to manipulation can begin with something as simple as the narcissist asking you to try something that you have not done before. When you voice your concerns and potential fears of what they are asking you to do, the narcissists may say something along the lines of, "You don't trust me?" "But it's fun, it's no big deal." "If you can't trust me and live a little, I don't think we should keep seeing each other."

These are just some of the manipulations that narcissists use when trying to mess with someone's head. For a manipulation tactic to work, it must be on a person that does not really know that is what is happening; someone naïve, perhaps not so sure of themselves, is the perfect target. Many narcissists look at people that have low self-esteem or may not be considered the "most popular" as easy targets. They think people like that should just be grateful someone is even looking their way. They do not often go for people that have everything already going for themselves; those who have the same amount of confidence as them, if not more, because they cannot challenge that person. In that person, they have met their match, and instead of petting the narcissist, always telling the narcissist they're great, and following behind the narcissist, they will set boundaries, and will not allow the narcissist to do and say whatever they want to them. A person who is sure of themselves has established their values and boundaries will not allow anyone to dictate how their life is going to go. Narcissists tend to have very rough relationships with people who speak their mind without fear. They are harder to manipulate and control. Those types of people are harder to get to buy the nonsense that narcissists are always selling.

The false lies and promises the narcissist makes are to get their victims to behave a certain way. Though a narcissist may admire people that are tough and confident like this, they may be intimidated by them, envy them, and so often pick an "easier target", someone preferably with little-to-no family, or someone that is estranged from family and that doesn't perhaps have a lot of resources.

Manipulation is one the biggest tactics a narcissist uses when trying to lure in his or her target. Not only does it include talking you in and out of things you would not normally do or putting on a false mask of appearance but it also includes talking you out of your possessions, your job, and family, and anything that makes you independent and happy. There are many instances where manipulation becomes a factor in a narcissist bag of tools but again once the veil is lifted and you can see the situation from a discerning eye, you will see it all for the manipulation that it truly was.

LACK OF EMOTION & NO EMPATHY

Emotional detachment and narcissism go hand in hand. Narcissists are not only capable of causing and inflicting emotional and or physical pain, but they are able to completely emotionally distance themselves from another person's emotions, and they fail to see just how sad or hurt someone might be from their words and actions. Not each person that may be considered a narcissist has this complete lack of emotion; it varies from person to person. There are different levels of empathy to be achieved, and a person's life experiences and hardships shapes that within them. Some narcissists are just a tad egotistical but can still tell if/ when they have hurt someone's feelings. This person still has some semblance and care for what is right and wrong.

There is, however, the other type of narcissist, the one that has absolutely no empathy, zero feeling, or sense of right, wrong, and remorse. This is a particularly dangerous person. If they have no regard for themselves or emotions of others, then that means they are more capable of risky, impulsive, and dangerous behavior as defined in the word sociopath. It can be difficult to maintain a relationship with someone that has little-to- no emotion especially as an empath. An empath's very basis is usually from a place of emotion and empathy. For example, when things get heated between couples in arguments, narcissists say things you would never dream of saying to someone, for fear of how it would make them feel. An empathic person would never want someone to feel that way, so the victim may be arguing, but it is with words of hurt, and they are just trying to convey their hurt and pain- even if they could have taken a better approach. When a narcissist is arguing, it is completely absent any sort of compassion, even wounded emotion. It is cold and calculated.

The words will have nothing to do with the argument. Suddenly, you find yourself defending accusations and remarks that the narcissist is throwing at you. They have you so focused on trying to keep up with the terrible things they are saying, you're so busy defending the atrocities and lies they are accusing you of, that it becomes a deflection from what you were trying to get through to them. Since they lack emotion, they say things that cause major shock value, and do not even care if you are in tears, telling them how it makes you feel.

Sadly, when you tell them that what they are saying is hurtful and untrue, or if you show too much emotion and cry, that actually feeds and fuels them, and they are happy that they think they have broken you. They are unemotionally attached so they do not care for your tears or your words nor care for severity in what they may have just done. People do not usually take pleasure out of making someone cry or hurting someone's feelings. That sort of person has a disconnection with emotions and human compassion. That is another reason this disorder is a serious matter and not something you just call a guy that you think is arrogant.

All they care about is winning. It was never about a resolution or giving you an apology, the moment the conversation turned serious or you were no longer happy with their behavior and you approached them about it, you were no longer seen as an ally. You are then the enemy in the eyes of the narcissists.

Narcissists do not like any sort of challenge to their authority, disloyalty, or competition which is again why they try and surround themselves with easy targets, fans and followers. They surround themselves with those that are more passive and enable and allow their behavior.

Now that we have thoroughly discussed narcissism and its many forms, we can briefly touch on how that type of person affects an empath. Remember, empaths are very nurturing, selfless, emotional people. They love to help others and feel on a much deeper level. They believe in healing and will help others to the point of exhaustion. That type of person is exactly what a narcissist wants. They love those that put others before themselves and rarely ask for anything. Those are in fact some of the very targets that they prey upon. Someone giving and someone that may "seem" easily manipulated and easy to convince and control. But when you know yourself and truly embrace your abilities as an empath and enforce boundaries, that is when you come into your true power and can prevent things such as toxic relationships and the like.

But we have not yet arrived at this time of awakening and realization. For now, this is the part of just understanding what a narcissist is and how being in a relationship with one as an empath can be emotionally detrimental. Narcissist's love to be served and empaths love to help and give to others. This almost seems as if it should work right? Match made in heaven. Hardly.

That is exactly what a narcissist thinks once they have found someone that is like that. When they have found someone loving and nurturing, they will swear they hit the jackpot all without truly valuing what they have. Even though someone may be giving, very kindhearted and unaware of their true power, does not give people the right to take advantage of that which a narcissist will surely do. They will eat that up and will expect way more from where it came from. An empath may be giving and selfless, but they are still people with very delicate emotions and deserve to be treated just as gentle and loving as they treat others. But in this world, it is full of takers and givers and everyone just must see where they fit in. Empaths often get the short end of the deal because we feel for others like no one else does.

With, maintaining a relationship with a narcissist all the while feeling everything on a very deep level is extremely hard but done often. It is not as if narcissists are selfless, they are not, so empaths rarely get back half the energy they put in the relationship, but the toxic nature of a narcissist can poison an empath mentally and even physically. Let us head into the next chapter and gain further insight as to why this is.

Chapter 4: The Slow Turn

After some time has passed and it does not take much, the relationship with the narcissists will begin to shift and change surely but slowly. It is now time for the narcissist to show you who they really are. The person you thought you were in love with slowly starts to fade within time.

Narcissists may start to ask for requests and certain expectations that they now have in the relationship. Things that may not have come up when you two were just getting to know each other. It starts off subtle hints of things they like and do not like. But then transitions quickly into always picking at you for something that you are doing and mocking your interest. But to truly have this power that they desire as a narcissist, they need the target to be isolated. So, they gradually talk you out of wanting to be around certain friends and family. The conversation can seem as if the narcissist is coming from a place of concern when, they just want to remove any influence and sense of help from around you. Anyone that may contribute to your opinion or anyone that may see them for who they really are.

Before you know it, you are suddenly convinced and motivated to see friends and family less and less. You come up with different excuses each time they ask if you want to go, and then there comes a time where people just stop asking. Some people are lucky enough to still have a couple close friends left that will start to notice the change in the victim's behavior. They will let you know what is different and often, many people do not heed that warning from loved ones.

They will just assume that the friend or family member is just being nosey and does not know what they are talking about. They may even take on some of the narcissistic traits that their partner has and begin to think that family is just "jealous" of what they have and they believe that they are trying to tear their relationship apart. By the time you look up some months, maybe years later, there is no one around but you and the narcissist. The relationship has now become very isolated and it can be very tough to even see what is going on from another perspective because you don't have any outside influences and or opinions to even point out that anything is wrong or different. It is now just the victim and the narcissist. Leaving them alone to fend for themselves and no one to lean on.

Once isolated, targets are more susceptible to pressure and sadly isolation is an easier environment for narcissists to treat the victim however they choose. Less eyes and chances that someone may uncover their fake persona that they put on around co-workers, family, and friends. By this point, with all the little changes and sudden expectations and boundaries that the narcissist now has on the relationship as well as any part of your old life slowly fading away, not to mention the loss of friends since you've met this person, it can all blend together and it can feel like a loss of identity. But in a weird way, it can feel normal. This is just now your life based solely on the "love" and manipulation this person has now put upon you.

Not all relationships that have serious issues must involve domestic and or physical violence. There are many where the relationship is a mental and character attack.

Narcissists are capable of making you feel as if you are nothing and no one without them so it can be hard to remember your true self, all that you are capable of, and what truly makes you happy. The relationship now consists of only making the narcissist happy so your wants and needs can begin to fade from memory.

While the relationship is still in the turning point, victims may notice a change in how they feel around the narcissist. At one point they were so sweet and loving and now the narcissist is turning cold and calculated. Arguments become more heated and disagreements start to arise more often and that is to be expected. After all, think about that dating phase and try and remember some of the promises made and façades put on by the narcissist. The impression that they gave you in the beginning of the relationship of how things would be. But that in fact was never the case. It was a luring tactic or a manipulation in order to get you to fall for them and quickly. So, when the victim begins to raise these questions and or call out the differences, they see that are causing concern, the narcissist does not react kindly or as if he or she cares as they once did. As they did in the beginning when they used to seem so concerned for our feelings and our emotions. But it was a mask. Slowly but surely you begin to see, as the relationship progresses, just how little they care or even have any emotion about it.

Things become more difficult not because the victim has done anything wrong or just "can't seem to get it right" which is a commonly known feeling amongst victims is to feel that it is their fault, but it is because things rapidly changed in the relationship and the victim has also slowly been taken away from anything that is familiar to them.

So, in fewer words, the victim is just trying to keep up. Their brains are trying to compute the sudden change, it's trying to figure out how the narcissist is so unemotional and unable to see this, and it is trying to still hold on to a shred of its old self, even if only a small portion. That is why the mind still on some or often occasions argue with the narcissist and or abuser. It has not completely surrendered and is still trying to fight, defend, and protect itself. Remember the person is isolated so there is also no one around to help, so all the mind and body has is itself to stand up for itself.

But that can easily lead to nowhere with a narcissist. They simply do not care about anything they may have promised or told you would happen; they may even ask or demand that you just do not bring up certain things and or subjects whatsoever anymore. Even if it is something that profoundly affects your life or something that hurts you emotionally, they do not care. Certain things about themselves they absolutely will not change and anyone who tells them that they may need to look at a certain pattern in their behavior or if you criticize their life in any way, you are now the enemy. Even if you are just trying to help or have the best intentions, all it takes is one wrong word or sentence and the entire conversation can fly off into very hurtful places. The narcissist will just think you are going against them, or do not trust them, or that you are disloyal and negative.

They will say that you are trying to change them rather than see the one thing you may be asking them to talk about that may be causing emotional pain. Maybe there is an area in the relationship that really needs to be worked on, but they won't feel like they need to do anything at all, and they'll put the entire weight of the situation on you.

Somehow, even though you are not the only one in the relationship, somehow, you will be the only one that needs to do any changing, or they'll say you need to learn how to adapt. It is all you. No apologies, no talking like adults even if the conversation gets heated, at least something of substance can be said out of that but not with a narcissist. Arguments are not "regular" arguments. It can just spiral into a verbal lashing. Not leading to anywhere but emotional pain and the conversation usually ends with the victim apologizing to the narcissist and agreeing to whatever the behavior was that the narcissist was doing that was affecting the victim just so they can "make peace" and end the argument.

These are all things that can come with that slow turn from happiness to the phase where the mask comes off the narcissists. You start to see things that are no longer what they seemed both at home and when in public. A narcissist is famous for behaving one way in front of friends and family and another in front of their victims. That is why when a person tries to describe some of the lifestyle habits and mental games that they are subjected to dealing with when it comes to being with the narcissist, many will find it hard to believe that person. The narcissist is just so charming and great at changing faces that they can fool many people into thinking that they just are not capable of such behavior.

This adds to the emotional hurt that comes with this transition into seeing the narcissist for what they are. Watching them act so differently, understanding, and kind to other people but at home they are so mean and distant to you. They are much less tolerant and patient somehow at home. It also hurts emotionally and is very mind boggling to know that you are the one that loves and tolerates their behavior and who they are, but they are nice to everyone but you. This leads into the next chapter when things really can turn for the worse as the relationship progresses.

CHAPTER 5: THE MASK COMES OFF

After the narcissist transitions into transforming the empath into exactly who they want them to be and after they have isolated the victim from friends, family, and resources is when the real person that they are shows itself. It can truly go from day to night. You never expect the person you love so much can be such a cold, calculating, methodical human being.

Conversations turn cold very quickly, and moments of tenderness and affection become less and less. In this stage, you are spending most of this time isolated and confused. Narcissists use punishment and silence as a way of retaliation for what they think is "betrayal" and or "disloyalty" even though the victim is only protesting the wrongs being done to them. Victims are not trying to cause discord or be disloyal but narcissists do not care about anyone's feelings but their own so even if you are just stating how you feel or pointing out behavior that affects you, they see it as you are bothering them and trying to change them. That you are just bringing them negativity and only seeing the negative. Even if it is plain as day that negativity is all the victim is being subjected to, the narcissist will not see it that way.

An interesting and unique situation to pay attention to during the slow turn in the relationship is around the time of holidays, birthdays, family events, important & special dates, etc. For some reason, narcissists are well known for always changing behavior right before a special occasion. They will sabotage any event that will bring you joy if it means settling the score about something or making sure that you don't have any fun that isn't centered around them right before the date so that just when the date or holiday comes, you are no longer motivated or bothered to want to do anything or celebrate that particular day. Have you ever experienced this? Where right around the time of your birthday or anniversary, the narc just seems to switch moods, suddenly there is an argument or fight over completely nothing? Or have they pulled the manipulating tactic of letting the victim know just how much they hate holidays and how much it is all a scam and that you are just being dramatic and wanting what everyone has?

Suddenly, during what should be considered a special time, you are left feeling alone and told to see things from the narcissist's perspective. To just leave them alone and think of this day like any other day. Which is fine, not everyone celebrates holidays and has different opinions based on religion, family values, and beliefs. It is also true, that not everyone is motivated on holidays and wants to bake pies and take pictures. But for some, those are very precious moments. Those are times they may not have gotten as kids and are trying to heal and love in their adult life with their own family. But when you find a partner that not only does not have interest in any of these things but purposely and what sometimes comes off as maliciously ruins the day just because it is in their best interest to do so, that makes it that much harder for the relationship to work and is even hurtful emotionally.

Suddenly your birthday, Christmas's, and thanksgiving are either less and less important or just become another day, you may even make a holiday dinner but it is not the happy and personal feeling you think it would be from your mate when they are a narcissist. Not that many friends and family to join you since at this point, the victim has somewhat been isolated with the narcissist. It is the attitude and aura of a narcissist both before and on the holiday or special event. It takes away from the joy you would also feel on occasions such as those. You are at holiday parades and parties alone because the narc did not want to go with you or if they did, some way, somehow there is just this awkward tension and attitude and they will begin to argue.

There are never any clear explanations as to why their narcissistic partners would just suddenly switch characters and begin picking a fight whenever they were trying to enjoy themselves with their partners on a date or holiday. It just seems to happen without warning and without mercy. They do not care if it is your birthday or any special occasion, some people are lucky to just barely get a call or a gift on their birthday from a narcissist. Their time is supposed to be preoccupied with what they want to be doing so if you are cutting into the middle of that, it does not matter the day, they will make that clear to you.

This may seem as if it may be something small or manageable, but this all falls under mental manipulation and or abuse. You are expressing your appreciation for days set aside for love and family because the world is always moving so fast that we miss those special times regardless of their origin, holidays for many, are a day off and time to be with family and or for reflection. A narcissist does not embrace the fact of family or love. The concept of selflessness even for just a day. This behavior can take a toll because they are ripping precious moments from you that you will never get back and they are moments that you are wanting to spend with them but they just will not see it or see past their selfish and negative perspective on life.

This sort of behavior becomes everyday life, sadly. It gets to the point where you do not know what to say and or do and you feel as if you are living in a minefield. Never knowing where to step, fearing it will trigger an unwanted chain reaction.

Remember, all friends and family have been removed, or only the ones that would have caused "problems" for the narcissist or in other words, seen right through them and would not allow their unacceptable and careless way of life. So, with no one around to help you see the issues for what they are or to tell you that it will not get better, a victim can become stuck.

It can be years before someone sees the true nature of a situation and realizes that it will, in fact, never change. But during all those years, a person can be weighed down by the narcissist. The longer you stay, the more damage that is done. Both mentally and physically. Narcissists are famous for gaslighting their victims. It is another horrific trait that victims deal with while in a relationship with a narcissist especially when their fake masks come off.

Gaslighting - *to manipulate someone by psychological means into questioning their own sanity.*

Behaviors that come with gaslighting:

1) Narcissists will deny they ever said something, even if you may have proof. If you do have proof, they will say something extremely hurtful just out of spite because they cannot say you are "crazy"

when you have proof. You backed them into a corner so now they will say the lowest thing possible to hurt you.

2) They use what is near to your heart, insecurities and information you trusted them with as ammunition to say you are crazy, unstable, or the problem. Or they use it against you in general.

3) They wear you down over time.

4) They tell everyone else that you are the problem.

5) Their actions do not match their words.

6) They use "positive" reinforcement to confuse you.

7) They project.

8) They are fully aware that confusion weakens people.

9) They tell you everyone else that ever speaks on them is a liar.

10) They try to align people against you.

Gaslighting is a huge part of being in a relationship with a narcissist, be it male or female. I grew up with two very narcissistic parents so believe me when I say it can be women just as much as it can be men. To gaslight someone, is like playing upon a person's perception of reality. It is a manipulation that is very hurtful and makes you madder to know that someone you love would do that.

To make you feel as if you are the one with the problem or they will completely re-write a course of events that happened and make you question whether you are sane.

Gaslighting is a form of abuse. That is why many people that survive such relationships come out of them questioning their every move and have major amounts of anxiety. They are afraid to believe in themselves. It is because they were stuck with a person for so long who told them what to believe, a person that would change history and events, would alter their thinking according to how the narcissists think, they've been isolated only taking in what the narcissists believe and values, they have only been told who they are from the narcissist. Told what to believe and when to believe it, because history and truth always changes for a narcissist. Whatever feeds their narrative in that given moment in time is their "truth" and they live in a constant state of contradiction, a walking hypocrisy. Narcissists practice none of what they preach.

When I say that gaslighting is a form of abuse, it truly is and here is another instance of what I mean. When someone is trying to express how they feel and are literally telling you about your behavior, the worst thing you could do is not only dismiss what the person is talking about but telling them that they are "imagining" things and or that they need to just accept who you are and your behavior. That is not realistic or fair to anyone or you if you have that sort of thinking. It makes you completely blame free of any abhorrent behavior with the escape route of "it's just who I am or always been".

That is unacceptable and would not be tolerated in the court of law as a reasonable defense so it should not be used against anyone in a family or civil situation either. Narcissists tend to show more respect and care to authority outside the home and those people do nothing for them. But those around them that honestly care, even authoritative figures in their own lives, they take them for granted and may not show as much respect for their feelings.

Gaslighting is also just turning the situation upon the victim. Or in other words completely deflecting from what the victim is trying to say and making it all about the victim. Making them question themselves, making them believe they are the one with the actual problem. Blaming them and gaslighting into now apologizing to the narcissist. Yes, that is indeed how it happens.

The victim will be so bogged down by the words the narcissist is using and the amount of mental manipulative energy coming through that they will eventually think they are the ones wrong and will apologize. This is abuse. Mental abuse. To always make someone question their own sanity with constant mind games and manipulation, to berate them until you get the answer you want is indeed abuse.

Narcissists are exceptionally good at influencing the mind and manipulating situations to their advantage. Making you see things from a certain "perspective", which is usually theirs. All those things fall under gaslighting. Playing upon a person's mind and emotions, using what they know about you to gain their goal which is overall control over the victim. They are willing to have these sad, one sided, emotionless conversation a million times with their victim if it means that they will one day just have them in the palm of their hand.

There will come a time in the relationship that you will notice that the narcissist only wants to have anything to do with you if you are always on their side of things.

When you are being "good", everything will seem to just flow and you will mistake this for real love or that things are getting better when in fact, you've subconsciously just realized how to coexist with this person without causing heavy disagreements. You may not see it on the surface but that is all that has happened. You know how those arguments and horrific words feel so you just do everything you can to avoid it which means living like a robot or carbon copy of the narcissists themselves. This sort of life is not normal or okay.

It is one thing to adapt to your surroundings, but it is another to completely surrender to your surroundings. Never give up who you are because it makes someone else mad or uncomfortable when you are yourself. That person clearly is not for you.

When you are waking up always pretending to be someone else for someone else you will eventually feel trapped and realize this. The real you will want out and soon. Who we truly are can only be suppressed for so long and no one should ever have to?

But those days that you "slip up" and say what is on your mind are the days where that mask is no longer there. All sudden out of nowhere again this person who is intolerant and unemotional shows up to snap at you once again over nothing. It never has to be anything serious with narcissists. They take any form of opposition as disrespect because remember they have a god complex so there is no room for any opposition to them. You want to start thinking for yourself and setting boundaries? Prepare to be insulted and emotionally hurt and to be cast aside by them. It is just what they do and that is why being in a relationship with a narcissist can be so damaging to the mind and soul.

THE BOND FORMS

Though there may be all this back and forth of good days and bad with the narcissist, there is something happening along the way the victim does not see going on. It is called *trauma bonding.* Traumatic bond occurs as the result of ongoing cycles of abuse in which the intermittent reinforcement of reward and punishment creates powerful emotional bonds that are resistant to change.

Victims become bonded to their abusers many times and many victims are reluctant to admit that on their journey and understandably so. Most victims fail to see and or do not want to see that they are indeed in what may be a mentally abusive situation because of the great amount of pain that reality will bring. But as comforting as hiding may seem, at some point, even if it is years later, we must see things for what they are at some time.

Bonding by trauma is not a healthy form of bonding. It is the victim becoming linked emotionally to his or her abuser, constantly seeking out ways to please them though nothing seems to be enough and coping with the punishment over and over again if they 'fail" or "act bad" in the narcissists eyes. Then when they are rewarded, they feel good again like they won the narcissist back when, the punishment was just up, or the narcissist just needed something. Nothing is fixed and that is how that repeated pattern of reward and punish bonds the narcissist to the victim.

The victim still doesn't understand that this is not a normal relationship, they think this is just a rough patch and that if they just change all these things about themselves, the narcissist will suddenly go back to being prince charming when in fact, he or she was never that person. The victim loves this person and does not understand the gravity of what is happening to their entire identity and self-worth. The bonding is only capable of happening because the victim cannot see that this is an ongoing pattern of life and wants to fix the situation which is why they tolerate the narcissist harsh words and careless behavior. No one would ever willingly keep getting built up and torn down just for fun or if they knew for a fact that that was happening. No of course not. Victims do not understand that it was never love, you were a mark. A target. A calculated mission that once was complete no longer needed extra attention. Sad, blunt, and true.

If people knew monsters before they got into relationships with them, I highly doubt they would go into relationships with them. Nothing is ever just obvious even if it is right in your face hence the phrase, "hiding in plain sight." So, with that sort of thinking, yes, many people stay and are unaware of the serious lack of real love in narcissistic relationships. They are unaware that any amount of time they gave trying to make the relationship work, has now bonded them to the narcissist. Every time they try to please them, to reason with them but still be the one to apologize, and each time they are punished and then rewarded, they are being bonded emotionally to them. Now each moment seems to be about making the narcissist happy and not doing anything to upset them or make them think you are unworthy of being with them and this is absolutely no way to live.

Trauma bonding is not only surrounding emotions but finances and resources as well. With no family and friends around and you are possibly not working or working somewhere you do not want to due to the narcissist coercion; you are now at their mercy in that area as well. Not only have they just completely taken over your love and dictated how it is going to go, they now have control over you in the manner of money and resources.

This is how narcissists like their targets. People that must depend on them so they can have something to gripe about when you are not doing everything, they want you to do in the relationship. They will always have this over you even though they are doing everything to keep you down from being able to flourish, they will still say it is your fault and it is just you. As if being in a relationship with a dangerous narcissist helps anyone advance emotionally in life let alone in any other way, especially if there is the concern and responsibility of children and others to take care of as well.

When you have no resources or money this is not something, they just hold over your head, it is also something they use as punishment. You have committed no crimes, you have not cheated, or broke the law. All you had to do for them to cut you off financially or make it clear that they are the ones with the money, is stand your ground on something against them. All you must do is disagree in a not so playful manner and see how much they care about you or your needs.

So now you are also bonded to them because you need them. They have stripped of you friends, family, connections, and resources. They've broken you down mentally so no they may not be saying verbatim "don't get a job" but they've made you feel like nothing, you are lonely, constantly triggered and depressed so it's hard to function in regular daily life at a job. They may have even told you directly that there is no need to work and that they'll take care of everything, another promise to always be wary of, but then in the very next argument, use it against you. So now the narcissist is now not only the reason you cannot or may have trouble working but they are blaming you for it.

Most victims go through this process. This is in no way, a way of life for a happy healthy committed couple. This is in every way, control. People think you must be downright in chains or have a glowing helmet made for mind control to see clear and blatant control and manipulation, but it does not work that way and these things are very real. They take place way more often than it should. There should be much more awareness of narcissistic and mental abuse. But it is one the most underhanded, hidden, and covert forms of abuse so it is easier to hide.

Once that bond is formed, it can be ridiculously hard to break. But it first takes seeing who you are and who the narcissist is for who they really are. They do everything for their own gratification and satisfaction. Once you start to see that, and there is no real love behind the words and actions of the narcissist, the walking away process can begin.

CHAPTER 6: THE MENTAL TOLL

You can see an obvious difference in a person that is in a happy relationship and someone that is not. There are just certain things you cannot hide even with makeup. You can't hide the sadness, the lack of sleep, the constant weight fluctuation, you can't be yourself, you can't be genuinely happy with those you once loved until you remedy the current situation standing in your way. Narcissistic and or mental abuse is a hidden, tactical, savage attack on the mind that no one else knows about except for the victim and the abuser. It is well hidden from anyone else so it can seem to the general public and or around friends and families that the victim is indeed the issue or the problem when in fact it is more going on behind the scenes than anyone knows.

The biggest thing of all is that it is not only hidden in general, it is hidden literally and physically. There are no "visible" marks or bruises. Mental abuse is not physical, though some relationships unfortunately escalate to that point. But mental abuse is all with words and the mind. Someone can be made to feel at their lowest, someone can take harsh words, isolation and anger, blame and punishment, broken promises, and personally built-in insecurities and wounds by the narcissist and still the narcissist has not left one mark on them. The victim wasn't hit once but every word, every day of isolation, every painful memory, every time you feel dizzy or weak, each day living in fear of what the narcissist will take away from you or say to you, is more than enough pain to endure and not have to be physically harmed to say it was abuse.

The mental toll from being with a narcissist is awfully expensive. But the lessons learned from that relationship can create boundless riches and happiness. We will get into that further down the line. For now, let's take a close look at the mental price we pay from being with a narcissist and or sociopath because falling into relationships like these are easier than people realize and can be very dangerous and steep to get out of.

Your mental health and peace of mind is everything and is something you want to always treasure. Well, think of it this way. When you are with a narcissist, your treasure is always under attack. You must keep it guarded and be on guard 24/7. Sounds like a lot, right? Having to be on a constant state of alert and on guard sounds a tad like anxiety correct? Yes, indeed. It is. Having to always be highly alert and conscious that someone you love is trying to get inside your head is overwhelming and for two obvious reasons. One, it is exhausting having to always do anything without a break, and two, it is mentally traumatizing when it is someone you love that is doing this.

Mentally, this sort of relationship also affects your identity and sense of self. You can lose sight of who you were and what you valued before you got with the person, the narcissist. Before they told you who they think you should be. When a person becomes disconnected with themselves in this way, they can mentally disassociate in other areas of their life, and with people they once knew they are now strangers. The victim is a totally different person now. They are a walking copy of what the narcissist wanted them to be mixed with all the new lessons and events happening in their life shaping this new identity.

It can be a very confusing and transformative time. You are conflicted by who you were, who the narcissist wants you to be, and who you are becoming. That can be overwhelming for anyone and what adds to that hurt is that you are having to do all this questioning and healing not from an enemy, but from the one you loved.

There are other mental hardships that are in play. The Post Traumatic Stress Disorder, the distance, the changes and insecurities that are now on you due to being with a person like this. You find yourself hating things about yourself you did not even notice until the narcissist pointed it out. Suddenly there is this new list of worries that you never had before, a new list of insecurities and all these things you need to change out of nowhere thanks to the narcissists. You are burdened when once you lived so happy and free. The financial toll, the family toll, the romantic toll, the depression and loneliness because of how much they make you feel alone even when they are right there with you.

There is the "third party trauma" that I referenced in the previous chapter, you not only experience this new strange way of life with the narcissist but you also have their enablers, friends, and family around all there to make matters worse. The family will indeed not know and or care how the narcissist is really treating you behind closed doors, but they also will not do much to help and will even make excuses for the narcissist behavior. They advise you to just do what the narcissist says or say that you may be the problem and they will add to mental abuse.

You are at a constant war not only with the narcissist but also with yourself because deep down you know you are unhappy and the real you is just trying to snap out of the mind games and manipulation but you're stuck. You're trapped between love and thinking you'll abandon this person if you leave because that's how they word it and make you feel, and being the person you know you actually want to be.

Here are a few signs and symptoms that may show whether someone is in a mentally abusive and or narcissistic relationship. These show the mental and physical toll this sort of relationship takes.

1. The victim apologizes a great deal
2. Paranoia
3. Self-doubt
4. Panic attacks
5. Exaggerated startle reflex
6. Isolation
7. Indecision
8. Brain cloud/fog
9. Disorientation
10) Fear
11) Confusion
12) Walking on eggshells
13) The victim puts aside basic needs and desires, sacrificing your emotional and even your physical safety to please the abuser.
14) Health Issues during tense conversations or arguments.
15) Victims develop a pervasive sense of mistrust.
16) Suicidal thoughts
17) Self Harm
18) Victims blame themselves for the abuse or begin to believe they deserve it. They also make excuses for the narcissist's behavior.

19) Self-Isolation

20) Protecting the abuser and self-gaslighting

21) Victims fear doing what they love and achieving success after years of hatred and doubt placed upon them by the narcissist.

22) Constantly comparing themselves to others and major insecurities

23) Victims will be reluctant to speak their minds and stand up for themselves

Overall, being with a narcissist has serious mental effects both during and after the relationship that if not seen soon, could have long lasting damage. As proven by these signs and symptoms you do not have to be in a physically abusive relationship to have severe lasting effects and changes to someone's life. Mental abuse is just as powerful as physical abuse. The words can be so vicious. Wounds may heal but the memory is always there, and words can never be forgotten. But physical and mental abuse are both terrible and unacceptable and you never want to have to choose between the two.

Narcissists do not have to hit you to show you that they hate you. The things that narcissists say and use against you can cause so much pain, including causing physical pain that can stress your health if you are not taking care of yourself. For empaths, during stressful moments and or arguments they can begin to experience an immense amount of energy swirling inside them and since arguments stem from negative energy, that is energy they are feeling in waves at that time and it can feel like nausea or upset stomach during the confrontation.

Does this sound like a desirable way to live or way to love? Of course not. Leaving a normal relationship and then leaving a narcissist is two totally different things. The emotional toll is much higher than when you are just going through a slight breakup. At least most people have emotions and do not mind showing them. They still care for you and may even still be friends after a breakup but not with narcissists. You are left feeling discarded because that is indeed what happened. It was not a breakup or friction in the relationship, it was just who they are and when they no longer needed the victim, they discarded them. Not broke up with amicably, maturely and like an adult. No, they toss away people like a kid that is mad that their toys no longer work. They throw it, break it, and toss it in the toy box. That is how narcissists behave and that is a very hurtful process to the victim.

CHAPTER 7: THE REALIZATION POINT

& ACCEPTING REALITY

To know there is a problem, you must first admit and see there is one. So many people stay in horrific situations be it physical or mental abuse and they truly do not see a problem with it. It is their everyday life. Even if they know they are unhappy, it is a sense of comfort in familiarity. Many people have childhoods remarkably like the relationships they end up in when they are older. So some thing or a situation may be unpleasant but it may also be something someone is "used" to going through and it just becomes a comfort zone, especially if you are in any way indebted or dependent on your abuser or person that you are in a relationship with.

In order to get out and ever live a peaceful life, there must be a turning point. A time of awakening if you will. Once that happens, there is no going back. Now, I do not mean, that you may never get back together with the narcissist, that happens all the time. When I say there is no going back, I mean that things will no longer be the same, at least not mentally. Once you see a situation for what it is, there is a sense of clarity that comes with it and things are no longer what they appear. It is as if the veil has been lifted and you now understand things in a much clearer light. With that light may come some shock, sadness, and discomfort. You are now seeing the person you love for what they truly are and that this is not a normal and happy relationship.

It is also sad because it may cross your mind that if you stay a little longer and do not give up, that things may get better. But that is a mistake, you must first realize that you are not giving up, you are getting out and you must also keep in mind that you cannot change anyone. You cannot make anyone do anything you want them to do or be who you want them to be no matter how much potential is there. Though every relationship has its problems, narcissistic driven relationships have a quite different emotional level of stress and discomfort. A different sort of uneasiness that can be hard to describe when truly in the thick of it and speaking of relationships having potential, that word is exactly how most people find themselves in these sorts of relationships so quickly and easily.

It is that "potential" that the narcissist makes you fall in love with. They quickly show you this lovely life with all this love and affection, and you're under the spell of thinking that this is the life that you will have and that does not end up being the case. But the problem becomes that you have seen the potential, you have seen what the relationship can be like if the narcissist really intended on making it that way but that was never the case. That was not their end goal. Their goal was to ultimately get you by their side, not make you happy. Knowing the potential, a relationship has and wanting that feeling back more than anything can be very costly. Because there is no getting that back. It was an illusion so now in order to break free from this you must come to terms with this fact.

You must understand that though it may seem like there is potential and it can be a great relationship if you just try harder, that there is no "trying harder". There is no figuring out the perfect way to make them happy and yourself as well. Because the victim being happy, is not what the narcissist wants.

So many people fall for potential and that can be a very misleading, damaging, and exhausting journey. At this stage of the relationship, you are tired of feeling this way. Of knowing you want more but not sure how to obtain it. You begin to see you are worth more and that maybe you alone are not the problem. Sure, the narcissist is not perfect, and neither is the victim. No matter what relationship they find themselves in, they will both have to work on something of course, that is the case in any relationship. But for narcissists, they have a way of making you believe you are the only one with the problem or problems period and that once you deal with everything, then the relationship will be perfect.

You may try different things before "giving up" such as counseling or therapy but many narcissists do not see therapy as useful because they do not believe they need any help. Not saying people who may have narcissistic traits do not go to therapy but it is commonly known that many believe they are above it or there are cases that narcissists will go with their partner to therapy just to manipulate the therapist and make them see what they "deal with" at home. They turn the tides of situations to their favor so therefore that visit to therapy accomplished little to nothing thanks to the manipulative charms that the narcissist puts on especially around people of authority.

Once the narcissist makes it appear as if you are indeed the problem and they've gaslit you into the very reaction he or she needs in front of the therapist while they remain calm and "centered" and appear to be in control, they think they've won. It is all a part of their plan.

This fits the narrative that it is you and now even a professional has said that you are the problem. Sounds convincing right? Sad that happens so often but yes narcissists use this as a convincing tactic with their victims often.

However, in these counseling sessions they will fail to mention the behavior that causes the victim to be depressed or lash out the way they do. Narcissists fail to mention the mind games, lies, cheating with no remorse or care, the "forced to adapt to their lifestyle" ultimatum they force upon you. The isolation and punishment, the harsh treatment for you and no one else. Let us not leave out the verbal abuse whenever accused of being exactly what they are. Yes, they conveniently leave all that out whenever they tell the story of what happened between you, but the truth will always prevail.

In cases like these, therapy may not work and so you try simply talking to them and begging them to see where you are coming from, but it only turns into a screaming match. A battle of words with no sight of an actual solution just hurtful words being hurled this way and that. You can only try so hard to get someone to see how they are hurting you before you just eventually stop doing it. After a while, there are no words.

There are a few statements and questions that you may find yourself asking or saying to the narcissist.

1) I would never do this to you or anyone else
2) Do you hear yourself?
3) Why do you feel this behavior or words are okay to say to someone?
4) Is this really happening?
5) I am a person too.

6) You cannot treat me this way.

7) You cannot say these things to me.

8) Why would you say something like that?

9) How could you say something like that?

These may sound like everyday questions or statements in any other setting but when you are with a narcissist, these things mean something totally different. They have a different haunting presence behind them. If you find yourself in a relationship and you must remind who you are with that you are human, that is a problem. A big one that I think gets overlooked because people do not pay close attention to mental abuse the way they do physical abuse because you can see one and not the other.

With a narcissist, you find yourself in conversations saying, "I'm a person too." Clearly you are feeling completely disregarded and feeling less than human and are trying to voice that obvious truth and they will not care. When words no longer work because they only lead to the narcissist making you feel totally unwanted and sad, you realize that this was all a show. A ruse. That you are only there for their benefit. Usually love would be a benefit for most people, but narcissists and sociopaths do not think like most people. You were there to serve and prop them up, you were there to pet them and make them feel wanted and always reward their mediocrity but that is not what you were put on earth for and that is not your job! That is why narcissists keep their victims around and break them down the way they do, it is to make themselves feel better.

It is quite hard, almost impossible to keep up this façade much longer when you reach a level of realization like this. You are ready to get out and get away with as little drama as possible, but it is rarely that simple with a narcissist especially if there are children involved. Again, they use anything close to your heart to get to you without having to lay a finger on you.

But at least and at last you have come to a happy place of awakening and understanding. Of realizing that you are much better than what the narcissist was presenting to you. If you have broken up with and gotten back with a narcissist, have you ever noticed how much better you do without them? There is no one around telling you how to think, what to think, what to adapt to, what to do in general. Your life no longer belongs to them and their toxic selfish ways. Yes, that is the life that awaits on the other side, but you must get there first.

When it is time to detach from a narcissist, it does not happen overnight or even peacefully most times. It is usually a long mental attack on the victim in order to get them to see things from the narcissist perspective and come back. Let us lead into the next chapter and see how it all works.

Chapter 8: The Discarding Phase

When you have decided that you want to leave this relationship and that you want more out of life that the narcissist is just not able to provide and does not think you deserve, expect problems to arise. The conversation that you think will be peaceful and adult, to say that you want to end the relationship, will not be peaceful or mature. Narcissists take great offense to being dumped or being the one left in the relationship. Their egos are massive but again they are extremely fragile. They will begin to lash out and not ask about any of your concerns to help make the relationship better, they will just immediately get mad and begin to verbally abuse their victim. They will bring up things from the past that the victim may or may not even remember and hold it against them, they berate them and make them feel like the victim is the one in the wrong for wanting to leave.

This is when you truly see them for who they are. When the breakup happens, the mask does not just come off, there is not one anymore. They lay it all on the line and say every horrible thing you can imagine and take heed to this moment because these are not words said out of emotion and anger, this is how they *really* feel now that you are no longer doing for them. A narcissist hates to be exposed in any way so when you call them out on this behavior and say you do not deserve it, that is when the mind games and sudden change in history comes into play.

They will say you either deserved those things or they'll say they never did any of the things you are accusing them of and that you are just creating drama and if you want to create it, a narcissist believes it's their job to finish and destroy it. Expect no apologies, no sweet outcome, or any outpours of emotion for a narcissist has little to none. When they see that you are really leaving and that this time you aren't going to apologize and then go sit in your room like a kid in timeout, they in that moment choose to discard you. Victims during this time experience some of the hardest parts about dealing with a narcissist because here is where everything they took from you will suddenly come into place. You will come to need the very friends and family that they took from you, you'll end up needing some source of income as usually narcissists are in full control of the finances and everything is often in their name.

Discarding is a term used in breakups with narcissists and sociopaths because that is what it feels like down to the core. It is not an ordinary breakup where we get mad and may block each other on Facebook after. No, when a narcissist discards you, you are made to feel as if you are nothing, that the time you spent with them was nothing, and that everything you did and sacrificed for them was for nothing. There is rarely a gradual peaceful breakup with someone like this. It is usually a fast disconnect from them and all their resources. They cut you off at the knees in hopes of weakening you and hoping you will prove them right in needing them.

Discarding can take form in many ways, one being if you were physically living with the narcissist at the time, then they can put you out with absolutely no warning, no help, no sympathy, and no emotion and no resources and it doesn't have to be over anything serious. If you do not want them anymore or accept a certain way of life and behavior from the narcissist, this is the result. Now if you do not live with them, then discarding can come in the form of just completely cutting you off in whichever form you had access to them. Be it internet, phone, etc. and if they were paying anything for you, that will be instantly removed from their concerns and you will be on your own to take care of it.

If you were in business together, they discard by normally taking it all from you unless you signed some sort of paperwork making it clear that you are a partner or key employee in your company but if there isn't any official legal paperwork or anything like that, they will use that to and lock you out of the business.

It can go on and on, just know any ties that you had with them will most likely be sabotaged after the breakup. Not every relationship ends with these exact results when it comes to being with a narcissist but there is an overwhelming amount of information in the world that points to the many similarities victims go through when being with a narcissist and the discarding and separation phase is a common one among victims as well.

When a narcissist discards you, it can be hard to deal with that truth itself. The relationship may have been taxing and hurtful all by itself but just the fact the person can just so viciously walk away and then not feel anything?

It makes you question yourself and you begin to wonder if it was really you that caused the issues in the relationship but that is common and false. You are not to blame and do not let the narcissist fool you.

Many of them may be heartless but they are aware when they come across a genuine heart and may miss the person they wronged so badly. But that does not change months perhaps years of abnormal and unacceptable, hurtful behavior. Again, do not let their confident appearance fool you, they are just as hurt and humiliated as they tried to make you feel which is why many quickly get into new relationships. During the discarding phase, many narcissists like to parade a new romantic partner in the victim's face. Little does the new person know that they are the new victim. Do not feel an ounce of jealousy or rage over this because you know what the narcissist is like and you know you did not cause them to be the hidden quiet monster that they are. You were not the first and you will not be the last.

They may make you feel like it was your problems and insecurities that made the relationship what it was and that their new relationship is so much better but that is a lie. Even if the narcissist is not fully aware of that. They can blame everyone else, find new targets, and lie as much as they want but they are indeed the problem. When everyone is telling you the same thing about yourself, you might want to start listening.

It can be especially tough being cast aside and then seeing someone else happy with the very person you were giving your all to but think about that. Remember when you were that happy? Remember he or she said the same things that made you fall for them? That is how it works with narcissists.

The new person is not special, they are just someone else and someone new to test their way of life on. Narcissists are also bored very easily, and their mind is always racing so they need new targets often to project these behaviors and feelings onto.

They need to constantly feed that appetite of being wanted. Not accepted, because remember they see themselves above everyone else and humans are beneath them, according to them, so with they are looking for specific targets as we discussed earlier. They love when someone wants to do something for them. They are ruthlessly selfish. So, during this process, try not pouring too much emotion into jealousy and pain. Yes, it can feel like a punch in the gut to watch the one you love with someone else but trust that is the best way forward and disconnecting from them will be the best thing that ever happened to you.

GO NO-CONTACT

The best way to truly get over a narcissist is by going full no contact. No trying to see how they are doing, or if they have changed. Because they have not unless they have come to understand that they even have a problem. And since major ego and denying ever having problems is a literal symptom of narcissistic personality disorder, let us just say it takes a lot for them to come to that realization.

Block them from your social media and do not look at theirs. Do not try and keep up with them or see if things could be fixed because during the discarding phase, the narcissist is in a very mean, spiteful, and petty state of mind. They are doing everything they can out of spite at this time. When a relationship with a narcissist first ends, it is too fresh, which is understandable, but narcissists tend to take it too far.

They will go from putting you out to taunting you about what little you have left and will threaten to take it away from you, they'll bring up anything they feel you owe them, they'll remind you constantly be it online or through phone that you are the crazy one, that you're nothing, and deserve to be out there without them, without nothing. They are extremely petty and vindictive to the point where they are only doing it to cause pain and not even out of emotion or sadness that the relationship is over. Everything they do and say at this point, to either you or someone you know, is tailor made to hurt you and name you as the bad guy. So, therefore I say and strongly recommend no contact when the relationship ends with a sociopath. They have no emotion or care that this is a rough and sensitive time for the victim. They now just want to cause as much pain as possible and get "even" with the victim for leaving them. This is the last thing anyone needs for their mental health while trying to heal and recover.

Cutting someone off cold turkey and starting your life without their unwanted influence is one of the best decisions a person can make when committing to leaving a mentally abusive relationship.

When you are driving forward but continuously looking back, you are at higher risk of a crash, but if you just keep looking forward and only look back when it's absolutely necessary, then you have better chances at arriving at your destination safely. When it comes to separation from a narcissist, you must completely leave them behind. If you did not learn the first time about who they truly are, you will learn the second time because each time is worse and worse. There is no "getting better" with a person like that. Not until they see themselves for what they are and look at the long list of victims that they have.

Chapter 9: Ways to Heal & Find Your True Self

It can be extremely tough emotionally to recover from any relationship let alone one that was filled with mental abuse and confusion. Nothing was ever peaceful and steady, not when you stood up for yourself or tried to input boundaries. So now you have taught yourself not to speak so much even when you need to. In that relationship you learned how to survive by not speaking your mind, by not having any boundaries, by just doing what made the narcissist happy regardless of how it made you feel.

Now it is time to heal that part of yourself. It is time to see the beauty and capabilities that you have. When you listen to someone you love and respect tell you for so long that you are not anything that you want or hope to be, you can sadly come to believe that is true. Going no contact helps with this very thing. You cannot heal if you keep revisiting the very person that makes you feel these things about yourself. Avoid attempting to get closure from the narcissist and or a confession from them to admit that they are indeed a narcissist. That does not normally end well.

Diagnosing a narcissist is inviting mental calamity into your life and wanting closure from them will only lead to more hurt, gaslighting, re-writing of history, and trauma that you don't have to deal with because you are no longer there.

Though most mature people can come together and have a talk about their past and what they could have done better and what they are willing to change, but not with a true narcissist. You will not get closure or an apology, not an authentic one anyway. This is an unfortunate occasion where you will have to move on without getting the words you rightly deserve from the narcissist.

Remember they feel they are very, very rarely in the wrong so telling them how they made you feel or hurt you within the relationship will only lead to them either flat out denying that, therefore making you heal that much harder, or they will say that is just who they are and that you are being dramatic. They may even bring someone new or old and say they do not have that problem with this new relationship they are in but that is only a tool to hurt you.

So, yes again for all intents and purposes it is best for mind, body, and spirit to just avoid trying to rehash old issues with a narcissist. It stunts the healing process and just gives the narcissist another chance to verbally break you down because you had the audacity to approach them about something that hurt you. That is not love or anything that you should return to. Talking to them here and there and flirting again may "seem harmless" and it may seem like you're back in a good space and maybe you guys could be friends but please don't be fooled by the very mask that put you in the position in the first place. All it takes is one wrong statement, a trigger or reminder of something that used to happen in the relationship and the narcissist is off again with some the most vile and harsh words you can think of setting your healing back weeks.

Do not give in to wanting to open communication back up with a sociopath and think of it this way if you are struggling with that or think it is too hard to do. When you are talking, flirting with, and accepting abusers with these behaviors, you are telling them that it is okay to treat you that way. You are giving them permission to do and say whatever they want at your expense. So just remember that when you think you are just having friendly conversation with the narcissist that did all those terrible things to you. You are telling them, "well, I guess what happened wasn't so bad." By letting them speak to you, you are giving them access to your space, your heart, your energy, and your mind which is that last place you want a narcissist. Always keep your mind safe around them because they have the power of mastery over the mind if given the chance.

Healing starts from within. You must believe that you want to heal and that you deserve better. If you approach the process through the perception that the narcissist saw you, it will be ten times harder to heal. You must try and delete their words and constant critique from your mind and that is a task in and of itself. Healing from a narcissist is almost like a reprogramming. You must be deprogrammed and reprogrammed. All the toxicity and negativity that the narcissist built in must be stripped away so you can now replace all the space with positivity, happiness, and light. You must get rid of the old, outdated, negative outlook on the world that the narcissist told you about and see it for the beauty that it really is.

There is counseling and groups that meet so others that have experienced something like your situation can come together and help heal one another. Sharing your story does wonders on the soul. There is this sense of relief when you share out loud what you have survived and your plans. There is a sense of happiness in wanting to help others overcome the same horrors that you did and you can even help them avoid it by helping others catch on to warning signs and eye opening behavior.

Another healing tool is positive reinforcement and positive self-talk. For so long all you heard were the words of the narcissist telling you what you are, what you want and don't want, and what you will amount to but you now have to start saying positive things about yourself out loud to rekindle the love and light you once had in yourself, for yourself and about yourself. There was a time where you did not know the narcissist and you loved yourself. Try finding that person again.

Search deep and combine your old self to the new survivor you are today, and you will have a superhero on your hands. You can take these sad events and turn them into a positive. Living in a narcissist shadow does not have to be your life. Take back your own power, love yourself first before you ever love someone else because you must learn to love yourself before you can properly love others.

OVERCOMING A NARCISSISTS

I have seen several articles and stories about overcoming the emotional waves of being with a narcissist, but I do not think it goes anywhere, in fact I think you are forever changed after dealing with a narcissist. You see things in a way you may have never thought possible in previous years, but they do in fact leave a huge mark on our lives. Now whether it is for the better is up to us. We must remember that we are the ones in control. The survivors must remember that we do not have to let people dictate how they behave in our lives and still control us mentally when they are gone. No, we must fully accept reality as is and move in the direction that makes us happy.

Like many relationships, when you are going through a breakup or already have been broken up and or separated, you find distractions and things to do to keep your mind off the hardships in that relationship that you went through, and while that is a fine recommendation for most, for victims of physical and or mental abuse, simply finding distractions and fun things to do will not suffice in getting over a narcissistic relationship. It will take time, patience, the love and support of others, and trust in self again. You will have to trust yourself and believe you can make it without them despite what the narcissist used to tell you because if you really believe that you need them and can't live without them, you will be right back in that unhealthy relationship with them or someone just like them. Thoughts, beliefs, and words are immensely powerful. Do not manifest the very opposite outcome you were looking for by saying they were right.

In order to heal and overcome a mentally toxic relationship it helps to also limit how much contact you come in with not only the narcissist but with their family and close associates. Or at least those that know the narcissist's behavior is unacceptable, yet they still enable them. Avoid those people. They do not need to know everything about you so they can then run back to the narcissist and tell them and then the narcissist shows up to interfere just as you were really progressing. Because there are narcissists that do not just detach from their victims, they keep their close fans, followers, and family to get that person as well. Keep your business to yourself, input and stick to your boundaries with the narcissist's friends and the narcissist themselves.

Make it clear with family and friends that you do not want to hear about the narcissist from them and they do not need to meddle in your business as well. You cannot detach and properly heal if you are still dealing with people who do not mind and enable the narcissist's actions and the ones that want to try and get you to stay with the narcissist instead of wishing better for you.

It is key to also give yourself time to grieve and forgive yourself. Forgive myself you may ask? Well, yes. See, oftentimes, victims and or survivors can feel like they are to blame for allowing the abuse whichever form it came in or for not knowing what they know now. They will blame themselves for not leaving sooner or seeing the abnormal behavior sooner and this is quite common. But survivors must be patient with themselves and forgiving.

They must also realize that they need not feel bad for not seeing an all-out attack coming from the person they love the most. No one would just see that coming and willingly continue. Narcissists are covert offenders and they attack the unsuspecting so do not feel bad that you were fully unaware of the danger you were in at that time. Release the constant thoughts of why you did not do or say more. Let go of it all. If you think about them in any way, they win and still have a mental hold on you and healing can take longer to manifest.

Lastly, be unapologetic about your newfound self-love and be happy that you chose yourself. For if ever given the opportunity the narcissist will always choose themselves so why shouldn't you? There is nothing wrong with being a tad selfish. If you do not think about you, who will? If you do not value yourself, who will? Think about your future and know the importance of boundaries now. If you do not have a limit, then the things that can happen to you are limitless.

The importance of boundaries is at all time high once you have been released from the prison of a narcissistic and abusive relationship. You now know what you will tolerate and what you will never allow again. You start your relationships off with more caution now that you have seen the uglier side of things and that is a great lesson to take with you on any journey. The lesson of boundaries, self-worth, and proceeding with caution instead diving in headfirst.

Speaking of moving on and diving in head first, when it is time for you to move on and try getting into a new relationship, do your absolute best to remove any lingering thoughts that the narc may have planted in your mind. Thoughts about who you would be in your next relationship. During arguments and heated discussions narcissists can hurl accusations and statements claiming that you are the problem and that no matter who you wind up with you will have the same problems. That all the problems in the relationship were your fault when that is not true and you have to be strong enough mentally to understand what you have been through and that your brain is retraining itself to see things from a new perspective.

You are not the problem, though yes, we all make mistakes, absolutely, and there may have been things that we could have done differently in the relationship as well. But know that you deserve true happiness despite everything you were told by the person that tried to tear you down and always go for your dreams, never settle for less than your worth.

Promise yourself to go forward that you will put yourself first and will tolerate no mistreatment of any kind. Listen to your gut and watch for red flags and know that one day you may be faced with the test of seeing that person again and falling back in love. Will you make the best choice for your happiness?

Take control of yourself, your life, your love who you choose to give it to. It does not belong to the narcissist just because they say so. You are your own person in your own right that owes no one no explanation for anything that you do.

We only get one golden opportunity down here on this blue ball we call earth and I refuse to waste it living for someone else, constantly doing for someone else, never happy for someone else, and definitely not under the control of someone else. This is your life! Treat every moment as such.

CHAPTER 10: (WAYS TO STRENGTHEN YOUR ABILITIES AN EMPATH)

To conclude this book, I want to express that there are ways to protect yourself going forward. Ways to embrace your abilities as someone who may feel a great deal but can still be empowered. Someone who does not allow every energy source you encounter affect you negatively in some way. And lastly, someone that knows how to love and give but with boundaries and strength.

First, give yourself time to heal as an empath and realize the toll that it may have taken on you. Accept that fact and embrace it because the more in denial you may be or the longer you put it off, the longer the healing will take. Next, research everything you can on the topic and become aware of your true self. You cannot truly know or love anyone until you know and love yourself. Knowledge for empaths is becoming more and more available as people awaken to their true purpose and calling and you can find the resources you need from books and online literature. Dive into what it means to see energy, feel energy, and what it is to be energy. Find how it all connects and will find the answers that you seek.

When dealing with personalities of any kind in today's world it is always best to take a step back and really look at someone, not their features but their spirit. When you become an empowered empath, you are able spot things miles away. Really look at yourself as well and work on self-confidence and boundary setting. Being with someone that has narcissist traits demands that you know yourself, it demands boundaries so practice that and when you are practicing boundaries, get comfortable in saying the word no and not feeling bad about it. Narcissist will walk over someone if they are unable to put up that shield of confidence and tell the narc "no" so it is very essential to be able to stand up for yourself and stand on any decision that you make with a narcissist.

I recommend studying and carrying crystals to deal with many different types of energy vampires in this world. Not only in relationships but for work, your car when in traffic, at your bedside, or just when you are at the store. Crystals and stones have an ability to protect you from certain energies and many unseen attacks that we all experience daily and again research can aid an empath on what kinds there are how to obtain them.

Lastly, for any relationship you are in, try to remember to fight hurt with love. Fight harshness with kindness. As hard as that may be when things are in the thick of the moment, remember that positive energy and reinforcement always outweigh negativity. At some point the greater good always wins.

Try speaking love and light into your partner and keep in mind that not everyone is a Grade A narcissist who just never wants to change. Everyone is fighting some battle or another and may just need a helping hand and kind words. No judgement, just understanding. Now with, never allow someone to just run you over because they may be going through a situation or they may be "unaware" that they are hurting you. Always protect and value yourself but also manifest a positive outcome for situations with love not adding fuel to the fire with more fire and negative thinking.

Give everyone a chance until they show you otherwise and as an empath, never let someone take so much from you, that you become resentful of that and lose the most beautiful part about being an empath and that is doing for others and having true emotions and feelings for everything in the world. Never let someone dim your light. You were sent to a cold world to heal and bring light and love into it. Embrace that and walk your truth unapologetically.